A Party
for the
Princess

Katharine Holabird

Illustrated by Chris Russell

Based on the original drawings by Helen Craig

PUFFIN

To Megan and Alison, with much love – KH

PUFFIN BOOKS

Published by the Penguin Group
Penguin Books Ltd, 80 Strand, London WC2R 0RL, England
Penguin Group (USA) Inc., 375 Hudson Street, New York, New York 10014, USA
Penguin Group (Canada), 90 Eglinton Avenue East, Suite 700, Toronto, Ontario, Canada M4P 2Y3
(a division of Pearson Penguin Canada Inc.)
Penguin Ireland, 25 St Stephen's Green, Dublin 2, Ireland (a division of Penguin Books Ltd)
Penguin Group (Australia), 250 Camberwell Road, Camberwell, Victoria 3124, Australia
(a division of Pearson Australia Group Pty Ltd)
Penguin Books India Pvt Ltd, 11 Community Centre, Panchsheel Park,
New Delhi – 110 017, India
Penguin Group (NZ), cnr Airborne and Rosedale Roads, Albany, Auckland 1310, New Zealand
(a division of Pearson New Zealand Ltd)
Penguin Books (South Africa) (Pty) Ltd, 24 Sturdee Avenue, Rosebank, Johannesburg 2196,
South Africa

Penguin Books Ltd, Registered Offices: 80 Strand, London WC2R 0RL, England

www.penguin.com

First published 2005

3

Copyright © HIT Entertainment plc, 2005
Text copyright © Katharine Holabird, 2005
Illustrations copyright © Chris Russell, 2005
Illustrations based on the original drawings by Helen Craig © Helen Craig Ltd, 2005
Illustration on page 1 copyright © Helen Craig Ltd, 2005
All rights reserved

The moral right of the author and illustrator has been asserted

Angelina, Angelina Ballerina and the Dancing Angelina logo are trademarks of HIT Entertainment plc,
Katharine Holabird and Helen Craig Ltd. Angelina is registered in the UK, Japan, and US Pat. & TM. Off.
The Dancing Angelina logo is registered in the UK.

Made and printed in England by Clays Ltd, St Ives plc

Except in the United States of America, this book is sold subject to the condition that it shall not, by way of
trade or otherwise, be lent, re-sold, hired out, or otherwise circulated without the publisher's prior consent
in any form of binding or cover other than that in which it is published and without a similar condition
including this condition being imposed on the subsequent purchaser

British Library Cataloguing in Publication Data
A CIP catalogue record for this book is available from the British Library

ISBN 0-141-31819-8

To find out more about Angelina, visit her website at **www.angelinaballerina.com**

PUFFIN BOOKS

A Party
for the
Princess

Books by Katharine Holabird and Helen Craig

Picture books
ANGELINA AND ALICE
ANGELINA AND HENRY
ANGELINA AND THE PRINCESS
ANGELINA AT THE FAIR
ANGELINA BALLERINA
ANGELINA ICE SKATES
ANGELINA ON STAGE
ANGELINA'S BABY SISTER
ANGELINA'S BIRTHDAY
ANGELINA'S CHRISTMAS
ANGELINA'S HALLOWEEN

Activity books
ANGELINA'S TEA PARTY
DANCE WITH ANGELINA
LOVE FROM ANGELINA

Novelty books
ANGELINA BALLERINA'S CHRISTMAS CRAFTS
ANGELINA BALLERINA'S INVITATION TO THE BALLET
ANGELINA BALLERINA'S JIGSAW PUZZLE BOOK
I WANT TO BE ANGELINA BALLERINA

Story books
ANGELINA AND THE BUTTERFLY
ANGELINA AND THE RAG DOLL
ANGELINA'S BALLET CLASS

Angelina's Diary *series*
ANGELINA'S DIARY: THE BEST SLEEPOVER EVER!
ANGELINA'S DIARY: A PARTY FOR THE PRINCESS

ANGELINA'S DIARY:

A Party for the

Princess

Dear Diary

Can you imagine what it's like to be a
real-true princess?

The Queen of Mouseland is giving the
biggest party ever at the royal palace in
Edamville – and it's all for Princess Sophie!
I've been reading all about it in the

Mouseland Gazette with my very bestest
friend, Alice. There will be parades up and
down the streets, tons of special
scrumptious food, brilliant singers and
dancers, and thousands of pink balloons. The
queen has even ordered the royal baker to
make a humungous super-cheesy strawberry
cheesecake — my absolute tip-top favourite!
Princess Sophie is soooo lucky.

There was a photograph of the princess
on the front page of the paper. She was
sitting next to Queen Seraphina in a

gorgeous dress, with a tiara so big it squished her ears.

'Can you imagine wearing that tiara with all those ginormous diamonds?' I asked Alice.

'Oooh, yes. I love anything sparkly.' Alice sighed. 'But that princess looks really grumpy. She probably wants sapphires and emeralds too!'

It was true. Princess Sophie was frowning straight at the camera.

'Yes, she definitely looks as snooty and stuck-up as Priscilla and Penelope Pinkpaws,' I agreed.

'I'll bet Princess Sophie's much worse than them,' Alice whispered.

'What do you think we could give such a spoilt-rotten princess for her birthday?' I asked.

'Liquorice whiskers!' shrieked Alice, and we both fell on the floor giggling.

Dear Diary

After school today Alice and I dressed up like Princess Sophie.

Of course we don't have any *real* jewels or tiaras, so we had to use our imaginations and pretend our old tutus were glamorous princess gowns and my pink plastic beads were sparkling diamonds.

We made our own golden tiaras with stick-on rubies and waltzed around my

bedroom, bowing and curtsying like two very royal princesses. Then we twirled round so fast we got completely dizzy and fell down in a heap.

'I'll bet Princess Sophie isn't fun to play with like you,' I said to Alice.

'Of course not, 'cause she only talks to other royal mouselings,' said Alice, rolling her eyes.

I pretended I was snooty Princess Sophie, and I ordered Alice to carry Mousie, pick up my ballet slippers and make my bed. It was really fun! Then it was Alice's turn to be a bossy princess.

'Yes, Princess Sophie. Of course, Princess Sophie,' I said with a curtsy, being ever so polite. I even tied Alice's bow and held up her ball gown while she waltzed around the room. She loved every minute!

PS We played so nicely that Mum took us to Cheddar Heaven for Cheddarburgers – soooo yummy. It's definitely our tip-top favourite treat!

Dear Diary

Today at ballet school Miss Lilly clapped her paws together three times – which means all mouselings must stop chattering straight away and listen. This is always very hard for my little cousin Henry, because he can never stop wiggling and squeaking for a second.

'I have a big surprise for you, my darlinks,' said Miss Lilly, showing us a fancy letter with lovely handwriting. 'My dear friend, Queen Seraphina, has sent me an invitation to Princess Sophie's birthday party.'

Alice and I gasped and stared at each other. We could hardly believe our furry ears! Henry was so excited he did a funny little jig, and Miss Lilly had to give him *a very stern look* to make him sit down again.

'But that's not all,' continued Miss Lilly. 'Princess Sophie adores butterflies, so the queen has asked me to bring four little dancers to perform the *Butterfly Ballet* for the birthday celebrations.'

Every single mouseling in the hall jumped madly up and down, squeaking, 'ME! ME! ME! ME! ME!'

Miss Lilly clapped her paws and said, 'Shhh!' until we were quiet again. 'Sadly, I cannot take all of you,' she explained.

We all stopped squeaking, except Penelope Pinkpaws, who nattered on about how her mother met Queen Seraphina once.

Miss Lilly handed out little slips of pink paper. 'Please write your names clearly, and put the papers into my special top hat,' she said. 'Tomorrow we'll find out who will dance at the royal palace.'

Alice and I wrote our names in HUGE letters and dropped our papers into the hat, and then we had to wait absolutely ages for Henry to finish scribbling his name.

'Maybe we'll go to Princess Sophie's party after all!' I said to Alice on the way home.

'Won't it be fun being gorgeous royal butterflies?' giggled Alice.

'I can't wait till tomorrow!' I shouted as I waved goodbye.

Dear Diary
Today was brilliant but also a teeny-tiny bit sad. Which part do you want to hear about first?

The bestest part was when Miss Lilly chose the very first name out of her pink top hat: it was me – ANGELINA MOUSELING! I was so excited I spun gracefully around the room like my favourite ballerina, Serena Silvertail, then Miss Quaver's piano got in my way. 'Eeeek!' I squeaked as I crashed into it. The piano made a funny 'plonk', and I fell flat on my whiskers. It was soooo embarrassing.

Silly Priscilla Pinkpaws sniffed in her

uppity way and said, 'Why are you so clumsy, Angelina?'

I scrambled back on to my toes (because real ballerinas don't give up, even when they make a little mistake).

'Congratulations, Angelina,' said Miss Lilly. 'Now let's see who the next lucky dancer is . . .'

Alice and I hugged each other so tightly we could hardly breathe.

'Why, it's Priscilla Pinkpaws!' said Miss Lilly.

'Oh, no!' Alice and I moaned together.

Alice scrunched up her eyes and wriggled her nose and I knew she was wishing wishing wishing she'd be chosen next.

'What a surprise,' said Miss Lilly as she unfolded the third piece of paper. 'The next dancer is Penelope Pinkpaws!'

Then Priscilla and Penelope skipped around the dance hall, shrieking and squeaking, 'Congratulations to us! Congratulations to us!'

They really are the most annoying mouselings in Mouseland!

Alice scrunched up her eyes, wriggled her nose and madly twitched her whiskers, all at the same time.

'Don't worry, there's still one more lucky chance,' I whispered.

I stood on tippy-toes and peered into the pink top hat. Miss Lilly's paw reached in and pulled out a very crumpled-up piece of paper. Somehow I already knew that this would be . . .

'Henry!' Miss Lilly announced with a smile.

My little cousin Henry was so excited he zoomed round and round Miss Lilly like a crazy rocket, madly squeaking 'HIP, HIP, HOORAY!' – and everyone had to leap out of his way.

'This is definitely unfair,' I said as Alice stared at the floor. A little tear trickled down her nose.

Miss Lilly said how sorry she was that so many of her special little dancers couldn't go to the princess's birthday.

'In our next performance, you'll be the first ones chosen,' she said, giving Alice a hug. Miss Lilly is definitely the nicest teacher ever.

On the way home Alice cheered up a little.

'You can send me a postcard from the palace,' she said, sniffing, 'and bring me a piece of that strawberry cheesecake.'

'Of course I will,' I said. But in my heart I felt really-truly sad.

'I'M GOING TO BE A BUTTERFLY, ANGELINA!' Henry squeaked as he hopped along.

'You'll have to act very grown-up, Henry,' I warned him.

'I'M NOT LITTLE ANY MORE!' shouted Henry. 'I'M SO BIG I CAN EAT ALL THE SWEETIES IN THE PALACE!'

'Please don't talk about it,' said Alice, covering her ears with her paws.

Dear Diary

Last night Alice helped me pack my suitcase, but after she left I cried until my pillow was soaked with tears. I already miss Alice soooo much – even though it's only been three hours and thirteen and a half minutes since we said goodbye at the station.

I can tell you that Penelope and Priscilla are not nice mouselings to travel with. They ALWAYS find something to fight about.

'I want to sit by the window!' Priscilla shouted as soon as we got to our carriage.

'No, me!' shrieked Penelope.

Then Priscilla yanked off Penelope's hat, and Penelope pinched Priscilla's ear.

'Yoweee!' Priscilla screamed, and the conductor came running.

'Has someone been murdered?' he asked.

Miss Lilly's nose twitched angrily. 'Mouselings who don't know how to behave will be sent home on the next train,' she warned.

Then she made me sit next to Penelope, who stuck her nose up like the Princess of Mouseland. (Ugh – she is just the silliest mouse ever.) Priscilla kept whimpering, so *she* got to sit on Miss Lilly's lap and have a pink lollipop – even after she'd been so nasty. (Imagine!)

I stared out of the window while Henry pestered Miss Lilly with silly questions:

'WILL WE GET THERE SOON?

'CAN WE EAT LOTS AND LOTS OF ROYAL CAKE?

'CAN I MARCH WITH THE GUARDS?

'DOES THE QUEEN HAVE TO WEAR HER CROWN TO BED?'

Miss Lilly's eyelids drooped lower and lower until they were closed, but Henry never stopped squeaking, even when she was fast asleep!

Dear Diary

Can you believe it? I'm really-truly staying at the Royal Palace of Mouseland!

When the train arrived there were two Mouseland royal guards waiting to meet us, and even Priscilla and Penelope were impressed. Henry was so excited that he marched after them, saluting everyone with his little paws. He looked so funny!

We felt very grand hopping into the gleaming royal mousemobile that drove us up to the golden gates of the palace. And the palace was even prettier than a picture postcard, with brilliant flags flying from the towers and beautiful rose gardens all around.

'WHERE'S THE PLAYGROUND?' squeaked Henry, but there was no time to find out, because we had to climb up absolutely thousands of creaky old stairs to get to our rooms on the tippy-top floor of the tallest tower.

(Of course, squeaky old Henry is my roommate – but that's better than the Pinkpaws.)

Henry and I peeped out of our window and guess what? We could see all of Mouseland! Then we looked down and spotted Princess Sophie in the courtyard wearing her sparkling tiara and a lovely dress with flowing ribbons. She was with a stern-looking teacher-mouse and looked very fed up.

'That princess is absolutely spoilt,' I told Henry. 'Look how miserable she is – even though she lives in this fantastic palace!'

Henry was so tired that he fell asleep with all his clothes on, hugging his silly old Batmouse.

That's when I discovered something terrible – I'd left dear Mousie at home! How could I forget my tip-top cuddly toy? I always sleep with Mousie, and it was truly lonely in my big bed in the tower without her. I sat for a very long time staring out of the window. I kept wishing Alice were there beside me. The two of us would have the best time ever in this palace, I thought. We could explore everywhere, and giggle about the silly princess, and play hide-and-seek. (We could even dance around the rose garden together!) But thinking about Mousie and Alice made me cry, and it was a long, long time before I could stop.

Dear Diary

This morning a horrible clanging bell woke us up for our first dance rehearsal with Miss Lilly.

'We have to get up!' I shouted at Henry.

We scrambled into our tights and followed Miss Lilly down thousands and thousands more stairs to the grand ballroom, where there's a big stage and lots

of gold seats ready for our big performance. Henry kept squeaking about how hungry he was, but I said he had to be a real dancer.

'DON'T DANCERS EAT CHEDDARBURGERS?' Henry asked.

Miss Lilly clapped her paws three times, so he had to stop pestering me and be quiet.

'We must all do our best to make this a very special performance, my darlinks,' said Miss Lilly. 'The queen wants Sophie to be happy on her birthday.'

(Ooops, I guess Miss Lilly doesn't know how spoilt the princess is . . .)

After that we had breakfast – but Henry wasn't too pleased with the royal porridge. I was very excited, but I had a few spoonfuls anyway, because Miss Lilly says ballerinas need breakfast to give them lots of energy.

Dear Diary

For the birthday *Butterfly Ballet* Miss Lilly has decided Priscilla and Penelope will be gold butterflies, and I'll be a silver butterfly.

'Henry is a little blue butterfly just learning to fly,' said Miss Lilly, which is lucky, because Henry loves crashing around the stage and always falls over.

The Pinkpaws are very proud of their golden wings and are always fluttering in front of me and batting my nose. (Grrrr.)

I miss Alice horribly. Today I wrote her a postcard and I even put a royal stamp on it.

Dear Alice
Miss Lilly says I have to be a
silver butterfly all by myself –
but it's really sad being a
butterfly without any partner.

The Pinkpaws are snooty gold butterflies, and Henry is a blue baby butterfly who can hardly fly at all.

Princess Sophie is so unfriendly she hasn't even said hello yet!

I wish wish wish you were here.

I MISS YOU TONS AND TONS!

Love, Angelina XXX

PS Palace food is definitely yucky.

PPS I have to sleep in a spooky old tower with Henry!

Dear Diary

The royal palace isn't quite as much fun as I expected.

At mealtimes we have to sit very straight in a fancy dining hall while a grumpy butler with droopy whiskers serves us. Miss Lilly has supper with the queen, which I hate, because the Pinkpaws whisper to each other all the time, and Henry can be very babyish. The food comes on silver platters, and it's soooo fancy – definitely NOT what mouselings like at all.

'WHAT'S THIS?' yelped Henry at supper, pointing at some gooey, white stuff.

'Camembert soufflé surprise,' said the butler in an icy voice.

'Just have a little nibble,' I whispered, but Henry shook his head.

Next there was shredded beetroot with mushroom sauce. (Yuck!) I managed a few bites, but Henry definitely wouldn't touch it.

As soon as we were upstairs, Henry complained that he was absolutely starving.

'I WANT TO GO TO CHEDDAR HEAVEN!' he squeaked.

Luckily I had some cheesy crisps from the train ride, and he gobbled them down.

But poor Henry wasn't happy for very long, and as soon as he had finished the cheesy crisps he burst into tears.

'I WANT TO GO HOME!' he howled at the top of his lungs.

'Don't cry, Henry,' I said. You see, really I love my cousin even if he does get on my nerves sometimes. And then, because I'm actually a very kind mouseling, I added, 'You can sleep with me.'

Henry immediately hopped into my bed.

So it looks like I'm going to spend every night at the royal palace squashed next to my squirmy, snuffling little cousin. It's not exactly a dream come true – and I don't even have dear Mousie to cuddle! Secretly, I'd give up my royal bed and the whole ginormous Palace of Mouseland just to be back in Vine Cottage, jumping up and down on my little blue bed with Alice . . .

Dear Diary

Miss Lilly says that we have to be very good and rehearse the *Butterfly Ballet* every day before we can spend an afternoon sipping royal tea with the unhappy princess. Miss Lilly is absolutely certain that our performance will make Princess Sophie laugh and smile – but I don't think so!

Rehearsals are very long because there's lots to learn. I love wearing my shining silver wings and a glittery tutu, and today Miss Lilly gave us special masks so we really look like delicate butterflies.

Unfortunately, Henry is more like a crazy bee. He buzzes all over the stage and falls right off the edge, but he never seems to get hurt.

'OOOPSIE!' Henry laughs.

I try to be patient and show Henry his steps, but he's not always a very good student.

'I'M FUSTERATED!' he squeaks, and then he just plops down on his bottom in the middle of the stage.

That's when Miss Lilly gets out her collection of 'little treats' and gives Henry some yummy blue-cheese fizzies – and he's as good as gold again. (How clever is that?)

But today Miss Lilly was very strict at rehearsals, because the Pinkpaws were soooo silly. They fight about the stupidest things, like who has the prettiest smile (they both have icky smiles) or who does the best arabesques and pliés. And they are always teasing and whispering.

'Butterflies are supposed to be graceful!' Penelope whispered, slapping me with her wing. (Imagine!)

31

Then Miss Lilly sighed and said, 'Darlinks, you must dance with your hearts – not just your toes!' (Well, you can't dance with your heart when you're busy being a horrid teaser, can you?)

Dear Diary

Some days it is no fun being in the *Butterfly Ballet*! I have to remember simply tons of things, and then I have to look after the silly blue butterfly at the same time.

'Follow me, Henry!' I tell him as I flutter delicately around the stage.

Miss Lilly says I'm developing a sense of responsibility, which is supposed to be a good thing . . . but I still wish there was another silver butterfly. The Pinkpaws are having so much fun being gold butterflies together, but it's no fun at all being silver all by myself . . .

Miss Lilly was VERY wrong not to let Alice come!

Today I saw Princess Sophie running down the hallway in a sparkly gown. She truly did look like a princess in a fairy tale, except she was crying. What could she be so upset about, I wonder? She lives in a palace and eats off silver plates and even has that special nanny called Miss Fidget just to look after her. And I'll bet she never has to tidy up her room or take care of a pesky little cousin like Henry. Anyway, all she has to do to feel better is clap her paws and tell Droopy Whiskers to bring her tons of Peanutty Passion ice cream!

Priscilla and Penelope have been nagging Miss Lilly every day, 'When can we meet the princess?' Miss Lilly says it will be very soon – but we must work hard at rehearsals first. (Ugh!)

We practise all day and have those big fancy dinners every night, and then we're completely frazzled and have to climb up thousands of creaky stairs to our beds

again. Even the silly Pinkpaws get so tired
they forget about fighting.

And the truth is, I really-truly miss
home, but I don't want Henry to know,
because I'm trying to be responsible and
brave. Still, it's really hard when you're
missing your very bestest friend every day.

Dear Diary

At last Miss Lilly gave us some good news. 'You've all done so well on the birthday *Butterfly Ballet* that I have a very special treat for you,' she announced.

'A CHEDDARBURGER?' asked Henry hopefully.

'You're all invited to a tea party with Princess Sophie and Queen Seraphina tomorrow,' Miss Lilly continued with a smile.

'YIPPEE!' Henry squeaked. 'THERE'LL BE LOTS OF CAKES!'

'It's about time we finally get to meet the princess,' said Priscilla. 'We bought velvet dresses specially for the royal tea party.'

Then Penelope giggled and smiled her meanest little smile. 'And what special outfit are you going to wear, Angelina?' she asked with her nose in the air.

'I haven't decided yet,' I said, but really my heart was sinking into my ballet slippers.

You see, I don't have a special new dress to wear to the tea party like the Pinkpaws. I only have the flowery dress I wore on the train, and it's not exactly fancy. I wish wish wish I had new matching outfits like the Pinkpaws twins. Sometimes life is definitely unfair!

After that I tried hard to be a happy birthday butterfly in rehearsals, but every time I thought about a dress for the party my wings started to droop.

Miss Lilly gave me two mint cheese balls to cheer me up. 'Don't worry, darlink,' she said, 'I don't have a new dress either.'

'I just want to look pretty, Miss Lilly,' I said. I gazed down sadly at my tutu – and that's when I had a truly brilliant idea.

Dear Diary

Today didn't start out too well. Miss Lilly told me off, which was really unkind – I only kicked Priscilla because she teased me about my old flowery dress. Then we had a truly horrid lunch of creamed Brussels sprouts (the worst!) and afterwards I was just too miserable to go to the royal tea party.

Then Miss Lilly decided Henry
absolutely had to have a bath.

'My mouselings must be sparkling clean!'
she announced.

Henry was really-truly dirty, and I had
to pour tons of shampoo on him.

'HELP!' he squeaked, disappearing under
the soap bubbles . . .

It took a long time to wash that little
mouseling, dry him and fix his polka-dotted
bow tie, and by the time he was finally all

clean and fluffy I was a soaking wet mess.

'HERE I AM!' squeaked Henry happily.

Miss Lilly smiled proudly at him and said, 'Darlink, you look like a little prince!'

Of course, Priscilla and Penelope had the prettiest, pinkest party dresses ever – with matching pink party slippers. They pranced around the tower spraying themselves with Honeysuckle Rose perfume until I almost fainted. Then Priscilla burst into tears because Penelope stole her hair ribbons, and they had a huge fight and ripped their ribbons to shreds. After that they had to share half a hair ribbon (which served them right).

'Is everyone ready?' called Miss Lilly.

I wasn't sure I'd ever be ready – but then I decided I had to be brave.

'Ready!' I shouted, and performed a perfect pirouette.

The Pinkpaws gasped and made revolting faces.

'You can't go to the royal tea party dressed like that!' said Priscilla.

Miss Lilly smiled at me. 'Angelina, you look absolutely fabulous, my darlink,' she said.

You see, I decided to wear my very best tutu and bestest ballet slippers. After all, they are my tip-top favourites, and I don't care what those silly Pinkpaws whisper to each other – in my frilly pink tutu I feel like the prettiest ballerina in all of Mouseland. So there.

Before we left Miss Lilly put on her best feathery hat and white gloves.

'YOU'RE AS PRETTY AS THE QUEEN!' Henry squeaked sweetly.

'Thank you, Henry,' said Miss Lilly. 'Now remember those good manners!'

The royal sitting room was absolutely ginormous. There were tall golden curtains and lots of fancy rugs and heavy furniture and silver everywhere.

Miss Lilly said I had to sit next to Henry and look after him (again!). But every time I whispered to Henry to be quiet, old Droopy Whiskers the butler glared at us.

Finally Droopy Whiskers harrumphed and announced in his icy voice, 'Please stand for Her Royal Highness, Queen Seraphina, and Princess Sophie.'

It was soooo exciting! The queen arrived in a silky green dress and an emerald tiara, followed by Princess Sophie and the royal nanny, Miss Fidget. I didn't like the look of Miss Fidget – she was the skinny teacher-mouse I'd seen with the princess before. Her teeth are pointy and yellow, and she looked down her narrow nose at us and scowled.

We all stood up and did our very bestest curtsies just the way Miss Lilly taught us. Then Queen Seraphina smiled and waved at us to sit down while Princess Sophie sat on her own in her party dress – which was silvery pink and even prettier than the Pinkpaws'. For some reason Miss Fidget kept giving Princess Sophie *very stern looks*, but the princess just kept her hands in her lap and looked at the floor.

'How charming to see you at last,' said the queen, and she nodded to Droopy Whiskers, who pulled a long golden chain.

As if by magic, servants in red uniforms marched in carrying silver platters stacked high with chocolate cakes and thousands of scrumptious biscuits.

'OOOH!' squeaked Henry, reaching out his little paw.

Miss Lilly was chatting happily to Queen Seraphina, so I stopped my greedy little cousin. 'We have to wait!' I said.

At last Droopy Whiskers served us, and silly Henry piled an enormous heap of cakes on his plate. Miss Fidget stared at Henry as he gobbled everything in sight, but Henry didn't care. I was soooo embarrassed. 'Remember your manners!' I reminded him, but Henry definitely did not remember any manners at all!

Then those naughty Pinkpaws twins jumped up and went to sit on either side of the princess as if they'd known her for ages – without even asking! Princess Sophie looked very surprised, but that didn't stop Priscilla and Penelope. They went absolutely mad trying to impress her.

'We have a very expensive motor car just like your royal mousemobile,' chattered Priscilla, 'but ours is silver with black leather.'

'Of course, we don't live in a palace like you,' said Penelope, with her ickiest smile, 'but our mansion has elevators so we don't have to walk up any horrid stairs!'

Princess Sophie gazed out of the window, while Priscilla and Penelope bragged on and on.

Meanwhile my embarrassing cousin Henry was now devouring all the biscuits as if he'd never seen food before – and pretty soon the silver trays were empty! Miss Fidget was definitely horrified.

'Sit still, Henry,' I said. 'I'll order more biscuits.'

I couldn't see Droopy Whiskers anywhere, so I tiptoed over and yanked on a long pulley thingy. Nobody appeared, so I yanked harder – and all at once the huge golden curtains all round the room came crashing down!

Everyone sat very very still – even the Pinkpaws stopped babbling. I didn't dare look at Queen Seraphina or Miss Fidget – I absolutely wished I could run away and hide!

Then I heard a muffled squeak. There was definitely a funny lump squirming beneath the curtains.

'ANGELINA, I THOUGHT YOU WERE GETTING MORE OF THOSE YUMMY BISCUITS!' squeaked the lump. It was Henry!

Suddenly someone started giggling, 'Tee-hee-hee-hee.'

I could hardly believe my furry ears.
Princess Sophie was laughing and pointing
at Henry under the curtains. 'That's the
funniest thing ever!' she gasped.

'ANGELINA, WHERE ARE YOU?' poor
Henry squeaked, louder this time.

I ran to rescue him, and guess what?
Princess Sophie ran too, and we bumped
into each other. How awful is that?
Imagine falling down right on top of the
Princess of Mouseland! Can you think of
anything worse?

'I'm r-r-r-really sorry –' I stammered.

But Sophie didn't care if she was
squished. She looked up and started
giggling again, and suddenly I got the
giggles too. Then we peeked under the
curtains together, and out crawled my little
cousin Henry, completely covered in
chocolate.

Priscilla and Penelope acted as if they'd never seen anything so disgusting (they really are the snootiest), and Miss Fidget coughed loudly and said, 'It's time for your lessons, Princess Sophie.'

But Princess Sophie ignored everyone and offered Henry her paw. 'Are you all right?' she asked kindly, helping him get up.

'IS THERE ANYTHING LEFT TO EAT?' Henry squeaked rudely.

'Shush, Henry!' I said, glaring at him.

But Princess Sophie just laughed louder. 'I'll bet you'd like some Cheddarburgers,' she said, and Henry was so excited he whizzed round like a spinning top. Princess Sophie turned to old Droopy Whiskers. 'Cheddarburgers, please,' she said. 'For all our guests.'

Before I could twitch my whiskers, old Droopy Whiskers saluted and marched off

to Cheddar Heaven. Can you imagine that?

Dear Diary

Oooh, I was so tired I fell fast asleep
soon after the party. But I have to tell
you some other exciting things that
happened before then.

Queen Seraphina didn't seem to mind
about the terrible mess in her drawing
room. 'It's lovely to see Sophie having fun,'
she said to Miss Lilly. Then the queen

clapped her paws, and before you could say 'Abracadabra' the royal servants hung up all the curtains again.

Soon Droopy Whiskers came marching back from Cheddar Heaven, and we had the biggest, best Cheddarburger feast ever – even Miss Lilly and Queen Seraphina joined in!

You can imagine how happy my little cousin Henry was – he tried to gobble everything in sight, but I remembered my best manners and took very dainty bites like Princess Sophie.

'Let's go and sit together by the window,' she suggested. The Pinkpaws made their most horrid faces, but Princess Sophie ignored them, and Miss Lilly gave them a *very stern look*.

'I hate being so shy,' said the princess, munching her Cheddarburger.

'You must go to lots and lots of parties,' I said.

'Yes,' she said. 'Big parties are the worst. I'm dreading my birthday party with all those fancy lords and ladies. Ugh.' And she rolled her eyes like Alice.

'Don't you want to dress up and be the special birthday princess?' I asked, admiring her glittery dress.

'Secretly, I'd rather be a ballet dancer,' whispered Princess Sophie, gazing at my tutu.

'Really?'

'Really-truly,' said Princess Sophie – and then something wonderful happened. Princess Sophie smiled at me, and she had the nicest smile ever.

That's when we started to be friends.

Dear Diary

After the tea party Princess Sophie had to go to her lessons with Miss Fidget.

'I'll see you tomorrow, Angelina,' she said, and waved goodbye.

When I went upstairs the Pinkpaws were in a very nasty mood. 'Angelina, you ruined everything!' shouted Penelope, trying to

kick me with her fancy new shoes.

'You made so much trouble,' Priscilla
sneered, 'and your stupid cousin got
chocolate all over the queen's best rug.'

This time the twins' horrible words
didn't bother me. Not one bit. I danced
past them up the steps to the tower and
leapt into my room.

I almost tripped over Henry, who was
lying on the floor.

'MY TUMMY'S BURSTING,' he moaned.

'You were a bit greedy,' I said, 'but you made the princess giggle and now we're friends.'

'REALLY?' Henry was so pleased he jumped up and admired his round tummy in the mirror. Then he yawned and curled up with his tatty old Batmouse, and soon he was fast asleep in his own bed.

Dear Diary

Guess what? This morning there was a knock on *my* door – it was Princess Sophie in a pink nightie! I was so surprised I almost fell out of bed.

'Shhh!' she whispered, with twinkling eyes. 'I'm hiding from Miss Fidget!'

Henry was fast asleep, and the princess closed the door and sat on the end of my bed. I could hear Miss Fidget shouting, way off down the stairs.

'She's always scolding me about my schoolwork and my table manners,' the princess sighed. 'I never have any time to play.'

'Can't you play in the rose garden?' I asked.

'Never – Miss Fidget says I might make my dress dirty,' said Princess Sophie sadly.

'But being a princess must be fun –' I began.

'Not really. I always have to wear fancy clothes, be very polite and do everything Miss Fidget says,' the princess explained.

The bell rang, which meant it was time for me to go to rehearsals.

'I wish I could dance like you!' Princess Sophie said as she disappeared down the stairs.

*

All day I kept thinking about what Princess Sophie had said and the way she'd looked at my tutu. (Can you believe that a princess wants to be like me?!) That night I lay awake staring at the stars forever, until finally I had one of my absolutely brilliant ideas. I leapt out of bed, tiptoed downstairs and tapped on Miss Lilly's door.

'Come in.' Miss Lilly was reading in bed with her pretty lace nightcap on.

'I'm sorry to bother you, Miss Lilly,' I said.

'Can't you sleep?' asked Miss Lilly kindly, putting down her book.

I snuggled next to her on the bed. 'I need to ask you something —' I began.

'Darlink, please don't worry about the curtains . . .' Miss Lilly said.

'I feel better about that now,' I said. 'But there's something else . . .'

'Oh dear.' Miss Lilly sighed. 'Are the twins being impossible again?'

'They're asleep,' I said. 'Anyway, it isn't about them . . .'

Dear Diary

Miss Lilly was so sweet last night. She listened to everything I said, and she's having a 'good think' about it. (It's our little secret.)

This morning Priscilla and Penelope woke up in a rotten mood and absolutely refused to speak to me.

Miss Lilly decided we all needed a day off. 'What about an excursion to Edamville?' she suggested.

'Yes – we need to do some shopping,' Priscilla replied snootily. She shoved me aside and trotted down the hall, saying, 'I'm so tired of my old clothes.'

Penelope scowled at the royal guards.
'Yes, and it's so boring in this spooky old
palace,' she agreed.

'PLEASE CAN I COME TOO?' begged
Henry.

Miss Lilly kindly invited him along for an
ice cream, even though the Pinkpaws twins
absolutely cannot stand little boy
mouselings.

'Don't you want to join us, Angelina?'
Miss Lilly asked. The Pinkpaws watched me
with squinty eyes.

'Thanks, but I'll stay here, Miss Lilly,' I
said.

'Good!' shrieked Priscilla and Penelope,
and they skipped off to the mousemobile
with Henry trotting along behind them.

As soon as they'd gone, Princess Sophie
peeked round the corner.

'Miss Fidget's in bed with the flu – I'm free today!' she said.

'I'm free too.' I smiled.

'Let's go to the rose garden,' whispered Sophie, twitching her whiskers. 'Follow me!'

She raced off down long corridors and through all sorts of fancy rooms with gold thrones and statues and mirrors, until finally we came to a large wooden door and stepped out into the sunlight.

It was so lovely to actually be in the rose garden at last. There were delicate pink and white roses everywhere, a sparkling fountain and a brilliant green lawn that was perfect for dancing.

'I'll show you how to warm up, and then we can practise a few steps,' I said.

Princess Sophie was delighted. 'Let's dance!' she replied.

*

We had so much fun dancing together
that Princess Sophie didn't want to stop.
We leapt over the rose bushes and twirled
round and round the pretty fountain. We
practised all the ballet positions over and
over, plus tons of pliés and arabesques and
pirouettes – until finally we collapsed
together on the grass.

'I've got a smudge on my dress, but I
don't care what Miss Fidget says,' Sophie

laughed. Then she smiled at me, stuck out her pink tongue and touched the tip of her nose. 'Can you do that?' she asked.

'Easy-peasy!' I said, copying her.

Then we stood on our heads without wiggling our tails, and by the time Droopy Whiskers arrived with a pitcher of pink lemonade, watercress sandwiches and pink sugar biscuits, we were the hungriest mouselings in the whole of Mouseland.

'This is the most scrumptious picnic ever!' I told Sophie.

While we were busy nibbling our picnic, two gorgeous yellow butterflies swooped through the air over our heads.

'Do you love butterflies, like me?' asked Sophie.

'Definitely!' I agreed, and that's when we decided to make our own special list.

What Sophie and Angelina love:

* We both love beautiful butterflies
* We both love fairy wings and sparkly tutus
* We both love Peanutty Passion ice cream
* We both love to stand on our heads
* We both love to touch our noses with our tongues
* We both love to dance – more than anything!

'I wish you could come to Chipping Cheddar and meet Alice,' I said.

'I wish I could too!' she told me. 'My parents are always so busy, and my sisters are away at Finemouse Academy, so I'm really lonely.'

'Is that why you cry sometimes?' I asked.

Sophie nodded sadly. 'I had the mousepox and had to stay home with horrid Miss Fidget this term,' she explained.

'I miss my best friend, Alice, soooo much,' I said.

'You're so lucky to have a real best friend,' Sophie continued, with a little sniff. 'When you're a princess other mouselings always pretend to be your friend – like those Pinkpaws twins.'

'Priscilla and Penelope are a real pain,' I agreed.

'Do you know what?' Sophie looked at me with wide eyes. 'Before I met you, I thought you were stuck-up and nasty too!'

(Me! Can you imagine?)

And then we collapsed in giggles.

Dear Diary

Today was the day every mouse in Mouseland's been waiting for – Princess Sophie's birthday! We had to get up soooo early to get ready for the show. My tail was twitching and my heart was thumping, because I knew something extra special was about to happen!

'Dress quickly, my darlinks!' Miss Lilly whispered as we all rushed to the grand ballroom.

The stage looked like a magic butterfly forest, and I could hear all the fancy lords and ladies saying 'Oooh' and 'Aaah' as they took their seats.

Backstage, the Pinkpaws twins fussed as they struggled into their costumes. 'My wings are bent,' Penelope kept whining.

Then Henry put his wings on upside down and got himself in a terrible tangle.

I was getting very anxious too . . .

'What if she can't get here?' I whispered to Miss Lilly.

Just then, the curtains parted and Princess Sophie rushed in. 'Miss Fidget thinks I'm watching the show with Droopy Whiskers!' she announced with a giggle.

Miss Lilly helped Princess Sophie into her costume. 'Good luck!' she whispered as she fastened Sophie's wings.

As the music started to play the two of us danced on stage together – and we were the two happiest silver butterflies

ever! Sophie had worked so hard to learn all the butterfly steps with Miss Lilly and me that she knew them perfectly, and as she spun and leapt across the stage she wasn't the least bit shy. In fact, we performed the *Butterfly Ballet* just like real ballerinas and did our very best leaps and pirouettes.

Of course, Priscilla and Penelope were absolutely thrilled to be dancing with a real princess, so they were on their very best behaviour. The gold butterflies were so busy flying after Princess Sophie that they even forgot to flap their wings on my nose.

Henry couldn't see very well in the bright spotlights, so I danced in front of him to remind him of his steps. Then Henry grinned up at me and twirled along behind the big butterflies without falling over once – I was really-truly proud of him!

When the show ended Princess Sophie curtsied with the rest of the butterflies, and then she took off her silver mask and waved to the royal audience. Miss Fidget almost fell off her seat, she was so surprised, and the king and queen looked at each other in amazement. Then they all stood up and happily clapped their paws,

and all the lords and ladies cheered,
'Hurray for the dancing princess!'

'What a wonderful performance,' said
Miss Lilly after the show.

Princess Sophie smiled. 'This was truly
the best birthday surprise ever!' she said.

Dear Diary
I can't believe the royal birthday party
is over and soon I'm going to see my
bestest friend, Alice.

This morning, Sophie and I filled a box with surprises and sweets for Alice, and the princess specially wrapped up a ginormous piece of her strawberry birthday cake.

'Please tell Alice this is from me,' she said sadly, watching me pack my bag.

'Alice will definitely be happy!' I said.

'I wish you didn't have to leave,' Sophie continued, looking at my suitcase.

'Couldn't you come to visit Chipping Cheddar?' I asked.

A little tear trickled down Sophie's nose. 'Maybe I can come when I'm older,' she whispered.

I could hear Miss Lilly calling, 'Angelina, darlink, it's time to go!'

Then Droopy Whiskers carried my suitcase to the car.

Princess Sophie walked beside me down the stairs, her tail dragging behind her. 'Goodbye, Angelina,' she said, and we hugged each other, while the Pinkpaws sniffed and looked at their wristwatches.

Just before we left, Queen Seraphina stepped out of the palace. 'Now that we know how much Sophie loves to dance,' she said to Miss Lilly, 'we'd like her to visit your lovely ballet school.'

Princess Sophie's eyes lit up and she looked as if she would burst with happiness. 'Oh, yes!' she cried.

'Princess Sophie could stay with me, Queen Seraphina,' I said ever so politely (even though secretly I was brimming with excitement).

Queen Seraphina smiled at the princess. 'That seems like a perfect arrangement,' she agreed.

As the mousemobile drove away, the Pinkpaws started squabbling about their hair ribbons again, and I looked out of the window and waved to Sophie.

'See you soon!' I called.

'Definitely!' she promised.

Then she danced off into the rose garden with a happy smile on her face.

Angelina's Dairy: A Party for the Prince

If you have enjoyed this book and want to read more,
then check out these other great Puffin titles.
You can order any of the following books direct with Puffin by Post:

Angelina's Diary: The Best Sleepover Ever! • Katharine Holabird & Helen Craig • 0141318

'Angelina is a magical character who fulfills every little girl's dreams'
– Darcey Bussell, OBE

£3

Not Quite a Mermaid: Mermaid Fire • Linda Chapman • 0141318376

You don't need a tail to make a splash!

£3

The Coldest Day at the Zoo • Alan Rusbridger • 0141317450

'The reader will be delighted'
– Zizou Corder, author of *Lionboy*, *Guardian*

£3

The Werepuppy and The Werepuppy on Holiday • Jacqueline Wilson • 0141319

'The truest true queen of fiction for girls is Jacqueline Wilson'
– *Guardian*

£4

Bad Becky in Trouble • Gervase Phinn • 0141318082

'Gervase Phinn writes with enormous warmth and wit'
– *Daily Mail*

£3

Just contact:

Puffin Books, C/o Bookpost, PO Box 29,
Douglas, Isle of Man, IM99 1BQ
Credit cards accepted. For further details:
Telephone: 01624 677237
Fax: 01624 670923

You can email your orders to: bookshop@enterprise.net
Or order online at: www.bookpost.co.uk

Free delivery in the UK.
Overseas customers must add £2 per book.

Prices and availability are subject to change.

Visit puffin.co.uk to find out about the latest titles, read extracts and
exclusive author interviews, and enter exciting competitions.
You can also browse thousands of Puffin books online.